This book is to be returned on or before
the last date stamped below.

000222

LIBREX

To Ken Brown
with thanks for putting up
with me. L.H.

Random House Children's Books

Published by Random House Children's Books
20 Vauxhall Bridge Road, London SW1V 2SA

A division of Random House UK Ltd
London Melbourne Sydney Auckland
Johannesburg and agencies throughout the world

Copyright © Laurence Hutchins 1996

1 3 5 7 9 10 8 6 4 2

First published by Random House Children's Books 1996

Printed in Singapore

RANDOM HOUSE UK Limited Reg. No. 954009

ISBN 0 09 968211 7

NERO

— The Hero —

Laurence Hutchins

Random House 🏠 Children's Books

"We'll help," said Sam and Dan.

Sam and Dan were very excited.
"It's our school play tonight.
Can you and Nero come?"
they asked Driver Jones.
"Sam is the hero," said Dan.

So they cleared the track
to the gate

and Nero blew great
blasts of steam to help
melt the snow.

They shovelled
the snow from
the hill...

and dug through
a snowdrift at
the tunnel...

as Nero blew out
even more steam.

On the way to the school
they met Mr Cox the plumber.
"What's wrong?" said Sam.
"The school heating has broken down,"
said Mr Cox.

"Don't worry," said Driver Jones. "Nero and I can help. May we borrow your pipes, Mr Cox?"

So while Driver Jones
started work on Nero,
Sam and Dan helped
Mr Cox to unload
his gear.

And then Mr Cox
went off to get
more coal for
Nero.

Driver Jones finished his work just as
Mr Cox skidded to a halt with the
coal, and all the parents began to arrive.

The parents went inside
to a beautifully warm
school hall!

The play was a great success.
Everyone clapped.
"Three cheers for the hero!" they cried.
"Thank you," said Sam...

And there was Nero, heating all the pipes.
"Hurrah for Nero the hero!"

Nero glowed with pride.

SAM

DAN